Michael di Capua Books

HarperCollins Publishers

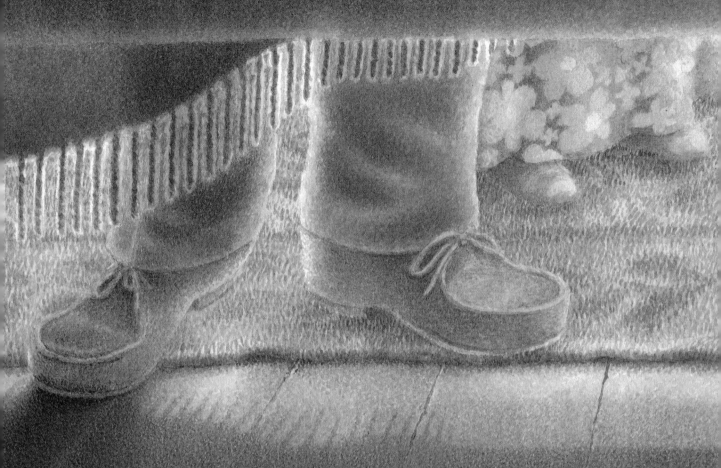

Toby, Where Are You?

Story by WILLIAM STEIG

Pictures by TERYL EUVREMER

For Lily and Peter
W. S. / T. E.

Library of Congress catalog card number: 96–85448

Printed in the United States of America

Designed by Atha Tehon

First edition, 1997

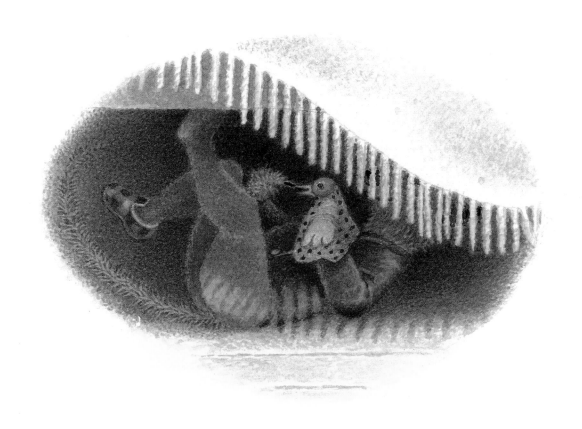

Toby has disappeared.
He's hiding again.

His father and mother are looking for him.
They're just a tiny bit worried.

Where on earth is that little rascal?

Is he behind Daddy's chair?
No.

Is he in this wastebasket?
N.O. spells no!

Is he up on the shelf?
No. Of course not.

Is he in this big pot?
Nope. Don't be silly.

There's no Toby
in the pantry.

He's not upstairs.

He's not downstairs.

And he's not outside.

So where the dickens is he?
He's got to be *somewhere*.

"I give up," says Toby's mother.
"Me, too," says Toby's father.

"Here I am!" cries Toby.

Toby gets quite a few kisses.